THE JUNGLE BOOK

by RUDYARD KIPLING

#3 Mowgli's Big Birthday

Adapted by Diane Namm

Illustrated by Nathan Hale

Sterling Publishing Co., Inc.
New York

Library of Congress Cataloging-in-Publication Data Available

10 9 8 7 6 5 4 3 2

Published by Sterling Publishing Co., Inc.
387 Park Avenue South, New York, NY 10016
Copyright © 2007 by Sterling Publishing Co., Inc.
Illustrations © 2007 by Nathan Hale
Distributed in Canada by Sterling Publishing
$^c/_o$ Canadian Manda Group, 165 Dufferin Street
Toronto, Ontario, Canada M6K 3H6
Distributed in the United Kingdom by GMC Distribution Services
Castle Place, 166 High Street, Lewes, East Sussex, England BN7 1XU
Distributed in Australia by Capricorn Link (Australia) Pty. Ltd.
P.O. Box 704, Windsor, NSW 2756, Australia

Printed in China
4/10

Sterling ISBN-13: 978-1-4027-4124-1
        ISBN-10: 1-4027-4124-3
For information about custom editions, special sales, premium and
corporate purchases, please contact Sterling Special Sales
Department at 800-805-5489 or specialsales@sterlingpub.com.

Contents

Happy Birthday, Mowgli!

Mowgli was excited.

Today was his birthday.

"I am all grown up," he said.

His friends came to celebrate.

Bagheera, the black

panther, was there.

So was Baloo,

the wise brown bear.

"Happy birthday!" said
Bagheera and Baloo.
They loved to tickle Mowgli
to hear the funny sound he makes.

"Do you remember how
you became our cub?"
Father Wolf asked.
Mowgli did not.

"I will tell him,"
growled Baloo.
"No, I will tell him,"
roared Bagheera.

"It was the middle of the night," Father Wolf began. "You were just a tiny cub," Mother Wolf added.

"You escaped from
Shere Khan," said Baloo.
"Who is Shere Khan?"
Mowgli asked.

"We have told you
many times," said Baloo.
"He is a mean, angry
tiger," said Bagheera.

"I'm not afraid of
a tiger," said Mowgli.
"Well, you should be,"
scolded Mother Wolf.

An Unexpected Guest

"Tell me more
about the night I
came," Mowgli asked.
"The other wolves
were not very happy,"
said Father Wolf.
"They were afraid because you
are a man-cub, not a wolf."

"I promised to teach you
our ways," said Baloo.
"I vowed to keep you
safe," said Bagheera.

"Safe from what?"
Mowgli asked.
"Hush," said Mother Wolf.
"He's back," said Bagheera.
"Who?" Mowgli asked.

"Run, Mowgli!" Baloo said.

"Why?" Mowgli asked.

Then he heard a low, mean growl.

"Take him to the den,"
Father Wolf told Mother.
"Give me the man-cub,"
Shere Khan demanded.
"He belongs to me!"
"Never!" Bagheera replied.
"We shall see about
that," Shere Khan said.

Mowgli Must Go!

Shere Khan sent
a message to
the Wolf Council.
"Give me the man-cub,
or I will come after you!"
All the wolves
were worried.
They called a meeting.

While the Wolf Council met,
Mowgli crept up behind.
He wanted to hear what
the wolves had to say.

"The man-cub is
a danger to us all,"
an old wolf said.
"No! He's one of us,"
said Mother Wolf.
"Shere Khan will be
back!" another shouted.
"Mowgli must go at once!"

Mowgli knew that the
old wolf spoke the truth.
To save his family and
all the wolves, he had to go.

"We will go with you,"
said Bagheera.
"Why?" Mowgli asked.
"We love you," said Baloo.

"We will miss you, Mowgli,"
said his wolf brothers.
They licked him on
his hands and his face.

They licked him on his knees
and the bottoms of his feet.
They loved to hear
that funny sound he makes.

A Short Jungle Walk

"Where are we going?"
Mowgli asked Baloo.
"Someplace safe," said the
wise, old brown bear.
"Where is that?"
Mowgli asked Bagheera.
"Follow me," was all
Bagheera would say.

"I won't leave
until you tell me.
Where are we going?"
Mowgli asked.

"Now, Mowgli," Baloo said slowly, "the first rule of the jungle is this: When Bagheera and I tell you something, you must listen and do just what we say."

"Why should I?"
asked Mowgli.
"Because we say so,"
answered Baloo.
Then he slung Mowgli
over his shoulder.
Bagheera tickled
his feet with his tail.

The three friends went to find
a safe place for Mowgli.
They left the wolf
den far behind.
But sometimes at night
the wolves could still
hear that funny sound
only Mowgli makes.